Written by Sue Graves
Illustrated by Jan Lewis
Designed by Blue Sunflower Creative

Language consultant: Betty Root

This is a Parragon Publishing book
First published in 2004

Parragon Publishing
Queen Street House
4 Queen Street
Bath, BA1 1HE, UK

ISBN 1-40543-007-9
Printed in China

Smoky the Dragon

p

Notes for Parents

Reading with your child is an enjoyable and rewarding experience. These **Gold Stars** reading books encourage and support children who are learning to read.

The **Gold Stars** reading books are filled with fun stories, familiar vocabulary and amusing pictures. Sharing these books with your child will ensure that reading is fun. It is important, at this early stage, for children to enjoy reading and succeed. Success creates confidence.

Starting to read

Start by reading the book aloud to your child, taking time to talk about the pictures. This will help your child see that pictures often give clues about the story.

Over a period of time, try to read the same book several times so that your child becomes familiar with the story and the words and phrases. Gradually, your child will want to read the book aloud with you. It helps to run your finger under the words as you say them.

Occasionally, stop and encourage your child to continue reading aloud without you. Join in again when your child needs help. This is the next step toward helping your child become an independent reader.

Finally, your child will be ready to read alone. Listen carefully to your child and give plenty of praise. Remember to make reading an enjoyable experience.

Using your Gold Stars stickers

You can use the **Gold Stars** stickers at the back of the book as a reward for effort as well as achievement. Learning to read is an exciting challenge for every child.

Remember these four important stages:

- Read the story **to** your child.
- Read the story **with** your child.
- Encourage your child to read **to you**.
- Listen to your child read **alone**.

Smoky the Dragon lived next door to Emma. Emma and Smoky were best friends. Every day, Emma went to the grade school.

To the
grade school

Every day, Smoky went to the dragon school.

To the dragon school

Every day, after school, Emma and Smoky played together. They played lots of games. The best game was when Smoky breathed smoke from his nose.

He made smoke curl and swirl.

He made lots of different shapes.

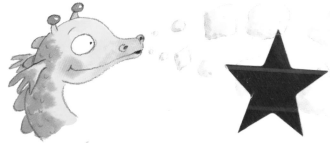

Best of all, he made big smoke rings.
Emma liked to jump through the
smoke rings.

One day, Smoky was sitting outside his house. He was sad.

"Boo hoo!" he cried. "I don't like school anymore. Boo hoo hoo!"

Emma sat down beside him. She gave him a large hankie.

"Why don't you like school?" she said. "School's fun."

Smoky blew his nose on the hankie.

"All the other dragons in my class are smart," he sniffed. "They can do lots of smart tricks."

"What tricks can they do?" asked Emma.

What tricks can they do?

"They can light fires. They can boil water. And they can make toast!" said Smoky sadly. "But I can only breathe smoke from my nose. Oh, I wish I was a smart dragon."

The next day was Emma's birthday. Everyone came to her party. There was plenty to eat. There was plenty to drink, too.

Best of all, Marvo the magician was coming to do some magic tricks.

"I hope Marvo will be here soon," said Mom.

Just then the phone rang. It was Marvo the magician.

"Oh dear," said Mom. "Marvo's car has broken down. Now he won't be able to come and do magic tricks for us."

Oh dear!

"Oh no!" said everyone. "What can we do?"

Oh no! What can we do?

19

"We can help," said three of the
dragons. "We can do smart tricks."

"What tricks can you do?"
asked Mom.

"I can light a fire," said the first
dragon.

"I can boil water," said the second dragon.

"And I can make toast," said the third dragon.

"Those are smart tricks," said Mom. "But they are not party tricks. They are too dangerous."

"I've got an idea," said Emma. "Smoky can do smart tricks, and they are safe."

"Will you do your tricks for us, Smoky?" asked Mom.

I've got an idea!

"Please Smoky," everyone shouted.
"Please do your tricks."

Please do your tricks.

Smoky did lots of tricks. He breathed smoke from his nose.

He made wispy smoke. He made lots of different shapes of smoke.

He made smoke curl and swirl.

Best of all, he made big smoke rings. Everyone jumped through the big smoke rings.

"Hooray!" shouted everyone.

"What a smart dragon," said Mom.

"Thank you, Smoky," said Emma.
Smoky smiled a big smile.

Read each sentence. The pictures
will help you.

Emma and  are best friends.

Smoky could breathe smoke
from his .

Emma gave Smoky
a large .

The other dragons could breathe
from their noses.

The third dragon could
make  .

Everyone jumped
through the .

Gold Stars reading books are for
children who are beginning
to read.

- Familiar, repeated vocabulary
- Short sentences
- Large, clear type
- Pictures that support the text
- Review activity